SILENT EARTHQUAKES

Poems

Poems by Tanya Parks
Photos by Peter Parks

Tanya Parks

Tanya Parks
StreetArtPress.com

Publisher's Note: This is a work of fiction. Names, characters, places, and incidents are a product of the author's imagination. Locales and public names are sometimes used for atmospheric purposes. Any resemblance to actual people, living or dead, or to businesses, companies, events, institutions, or locales is completely coincidental.

Silent Earthquakes / Tanya Parks. -- 1st ed.
ISBN 978-0-5788149-0-2

Many thanks to my dear husband and son! Without their help this never would have been finished. Much love! TP

Contents

ONE

TWO

THREE

ONE

LOOK 15 PP 2020

Awake

Who was it
that painted
this heart?
And what was it
about this morning
that led me to find
an inner lake of golden light? What keeps these
winter birds
alive through the night
so that we may watch the dawn together
on this day
unlike any other?

To-Do List

Here we are
and it's all of it.
I wake up falling out of dreams to say
thank you
for depositing me here.
All I have to do today
is live.

11/13/2020

On this day of power
link arms with your positive intentions
and release your negative ones
to the sky.

Fight for the self
that dares creation
the part of you that is boundless
full of color and dimension.

Don't be stalled by the negative
let hate fall where it rose
call in the healing light
the leaves rustling
an ancient song
as you go.

LOOK 1B PP 2020

Silent earthquakes

Endings happen
ready or not
you can feel the drum beat
as the seasons change

With deep tremors
the ground begins to slip
following its own course
the kaleidoscope of matter.

Fifty miles below
plates stretch and melt
an inferno of the elements

a magnitude six realizing
breaking, releasing.

In fire and crushing force
we watch this dream
having been pulled from ether and lived

waving, diving the years, the mountain
returning to the mantle.

This life has grown into something new
always toward the sun
so we get back on the road
our voices now a memory
in these old adobe walls.

Goodbye valley.
We won't have the strength to return
yet we're made of this earth
after all these years, and this sky.

The truth says
were moving on again,
heading north
to a place where there's
always silent earthquakes.

LOOK 21 FP 2020

Meditation

You wail and plead
now stop
and listen.
Search for the answers

trying to reach you
feel the replies.

Listen as intently
as when on the moonless path
your whole being turning to hear.

LOOK 2 FP 2020

Not the black bead or the white bead

If it's going all to hell
and I end up in it
I'll make the most of things

Yeah, he said
but you're there NOW.
What are you going to do about it?

Maybe it's enough
to just do what you do, to walk up and feed the
birds on a freezing morning in January.
Maybe that's enough of an act
to save the world.

I hang on, determined to keep standing
while all around fall the ashes, proof
of an ending, of a whole world
our life together.

Now on the other side of that door

sitting with the finality of its statement -
there's no other way than off this step -
yet all directions show nothing but mist.

I knew it all once
who was that person?
Now, I'm falling down the well.
You'll have to rely on your sensibilities.

LOOK 13 PP 2020

On the heels of an ending

In the dream
I'm walking toward the square
of a cobblestone town
and hear it happen
but cannot see
the old life leap to its death.
People rush past toward the scene.
I turn in anxiety to see
if the new life is safe,
and this is represented
by a baby so fat and sweet and smiling how could I
not let go
of what is over and done?
I have lived it
we have loved each other,
it cannot be taken away.
And this lets me wake
and move on.

A member of the multitude

On the morning bus
everyone hides in their hoods

I read a poem about
not being able to save anybody,
and how sometimes the words that come
are not reassuring.

Looking out the window at the rain, driving
through a thousand years and knowing
this is all right.

The trials sit beside us
helping us understand.

Oh love
no one knows the story but you.

Questions

What do you want me to know today
I ask the sky -
Chill out and relax a little,
you don't have to know everything.

In the backroom I realize
my face represents
what I cannot outrun
and will not likely forgive.

What should I do with this information
I ask the blue -
Give me a break, give yourself a break
things are tough all over.

During the day I see
there's nothing to me
but habits and assumptions.
Crossing bridge they blow away.

LOOK 11 PP 2020

No effort

No longer looking to crowd my emptiness
with the noise of effort

I am still.

No longer looking to be something
do something, make something
I can hear what is.
(it's very quiet)

The sad and lonely place in me
breathes a sigh of relief
and sticks its head out

for the first time
not fearing to be crushed
by a falling book.

It takes remembering
we're all the same light
to stay in this place
of flowing non resistance

No sense thinking now -
I step out to the windblown field.

More notes to self

Resist mediocrity and bitterness
fight for compassion and calm
reject confusion and helplessness
don't be a jerk.

Talk it out with the birds
find your answers in the woods.
Insist on gardens!
Indulge in walks.
Smile at your child.

It takes courage to
look up and keep going.
Sometimes the fear takes over but know
you're made for this world.

Allow for currents
you are not in danger.

LOOK 6 PP 2020

11/11/15

We have come and gone
in this life
and what of it?

We've loved when young
we've loved when old.

I list the dead, then fall asleep
in the middle of it.

I'm re arranging a nursery
to accommodate more cribs
it's going to be big!

7 baby beds?
I wake up -
making room for new ideas

the cold dawn is standing
just outside the door

peeking in, whispering about
snow coming.

What do you want your life to be about?
A voice kept asking yesterday -
What do you want your LIFE
to be about?

As if we could
structure such a thing
or can we?

It seems no matter what costume wear
it's is obvious, the flame within.
Behind the hat, behind the gray, it radiates
our luminous nature.

The ravens shout
and it's morning.

TWO

LOOK 16 PP 2020

The long slow process of being pulled apart

At night
there is hail on the roof
and the endless milky way
all stars, constellations
are hidden now by winter clouds.
Its 4 and I've slept enough.
My hands in the kitchen light
look so worn and I know
my time is limited.

I can't quite
understand, but feel
we are slowly being
pulled apart.
Broken into pieces
and thrown to the winds. Just because
we've been given a

miracle doesn’t mean
we get to keep it.

I wish there was
some way love
to illustrate no separation
but all we have
is our blood understanding
of a life spent together.
This is how we’ll stay in touch.

Last night, the coyotes
came back. A big
pack of them and
sang all around the house -
I haven’t heard them in so long!

And they talked
about the cold winter
and the longing of life
and changes
coming.

$5 poem

Here it is day
And the mountain appears.
The bees are in the grass
and the boats slip around.

At the end of all our effort, he takes a hit
the smoke rising in lieu of incense.

There is no inside.
There is no self.
Thank you August
for receiving us.

LOOK 3B PP 2020

Halfway thru a life, or something

I wake up
and remember who and what I am.
That heavy loathing never more
than an eyelid away.

My chest feels crushed.
This body cant withstand
this negative mind.

Was it me
who bestowed the crooked legacy
by accepting the madness?
All this time standing in the broken lack
an angry impatience, a personal werewolf
for what?

Let go the linear mind myth
take all the time you need to discover patience.
The only way to let this pain
roll out on its own.

The only way to forgiveness,
if you're lucky.

I sit here thinking
to feel like a failure of a person
is an invitation to distortion.
I must release everything
and remember what I'd do
if I were doing it for you.

The riddle is: short of death
how does one
become as wide and clear as the desert sky -
holding everything and yet everything's free

These are the things on my mind
while trying to figure out
is it possible to
wake up once and
let the first thought be for peace.

LOOK 32 PP 2020

Begin again

I put down my hands
as useless
and continue into the void
listening for the calls.

What if we just gave ourselves up
to the flow of what is?
relaxing with no direction
brings the moonlight from the cloud

Terror still comes
but there's a part of me
that stands to one side, knowing
it's not the last word.

Silver water, white sky

Swarms of birds
race along the beach.
Two flocks becoming one expanding, rising
stringing out
a ribbon, now a ball
suddenly falling
into the shape of one bird.
Things are changing
that fast
that's how
it needs to be
so don't
hold on to the thought.

Having entered this door

Life is in the street and life is in the fields
my mind is in the light
my thoughts are on the mantra.
Believe what says the heart
mine has flown here
or have we never moved
and your dream of me
has met my dream of you.
To be in a state
of letting go is to live the silence.
To be with you - incredible fortune!
makes me so thankful
for living.

Win or lose

Standing while on break

inside by the window
shivering because it's cold in here and out there.

The masked passersby hustle
below on the street and I'm
just another person working in the city.

In my mind
drifting in beside you, warmth covers me
darkness protects me.

What will become of us?
Will we make it through another year? The answer
doesn't matter
just write another line.

LOOK 5 PP 2020

Growth in November

Today's page looked up and said 'Go away'.
Or, what there was to say ran off in the grass that grows in the city.

How can I consider myself lost in the world
if the whole thing hums
in the palm of your hand?

A part of me stays there, watching the river.

Silence has come to the city

A few weeks ago
a door closed on the world and a sign was put up
Contamination Line - Do Not Cross.

Now we make our way downtown at dawn on a
Monday and the streets are inhabited
by dim light only.

Look at that you say
if we make it through this you'll never see the like
again. So I take a picture,
as I intend to make it
and see with you
what's on the other side.

Impermanence means
this too is in motion.
So we raise our vibrations now to meet this new
life where it is, in the heart, on the street
in the silence.

LOOK 2 PP 2020

Guidelines

If I can
learn to take care
of the one,
then I will always be caring
for the many.
If it's habit to
be kind to the one,
then I will be
like this
consciously
with the many.
In life, in death, in dream.
If you only get
one good idea a day
use it.

In the night

In the night
the streets are quiet
as a quarantine from death
is attempted.
Have I
already made my peace with this?
I turn my face up
into the falling rain -
it increases the more I laugh!
A downpour of blessings
arriving without effort,
this is how life can be.

LOOK 22 PP 2020

Every year

Every year its more apparent we're dying
so formality is losing its place
like a self-imposed rule
swallowed in another life
the reason now lost to childhood streets
understood only by faces you will never see again
and the Christmas cards that are a poem
won't be coming this year
because the author is dead
so I will take up the thread
I will take it up.

I want to say that every year
ignorance is burned off a little more
the curtain has lifted
and I am hushed by your fragile humanity
and must be intentionally loving
polite, gentle
careful with whats disturbed.

We are responsible for each other
so these hands are charged with healing.

I see that walking the talk has arrived at my door
and I must lean on my beliefs now
...the empty form, the formless emptiness...
don't give up, use this time, use it
for even though this experience is finite
this moment is a timeless entity.
This vision can be a good one
with the light expanding from within us
continuing beyond us.

Don't give up on living!
there's still revelations to come
like how 30 years from now
you'll be so
like I'm so thankful
for another chance to be a human being.

LOOK 34 PP 2021

THREE

LOOK 23 PP 2020

Receive

I radiate light
I am the light
the mere thought of my guides makes it so.
Slowly, slowly I walk through this plane
releasing attachment to outcome, allowing the
ships to come in. Slowly untangled from doubt
I am released
through following the way
I am free.
Pain you schooled me -
cleared the deck.
Now I'm just
full of love
having gained the courage
to just let the good things come.

Ground zero

Sitting upright
I am immersed
dissolved in the mystery.

My inner and outer being flash like a school of fish
changing direction.

The whole world has been told to stay home
standing everything
on its head.

Will we learn to evolve now
seeing through duality
using our own power to heal.

Will we realize
the truth of what's happening
and commit to each other endlessly.

LOOK 28 PP 2020

In love

Sometimes
it's all
about to break
the wall has materialized
and gravity has increased.
Then you appear - what is this
song only your heart sings to mine?
The oceans unfreeze and
we kick that
can all the
way down the road.

Divine timing

Everyone is learning how
to get quiet
whether we want to
or not
and experience the stillness
like morning air in the desert.
It's your birthday in lockdown
and what would you be doing
otherwise? Celebrate life,
dance where you are,
you are so loved
try to understand that
and let it be enough.

What it is

I try to sit with you
mornings
and tell you how I feel
it's not that it's one sided
but I have no patience to wait
for the reply
so we get together in other ways.
You drag me out of the ditch
by my shirt,
I lift you out of the sink
with a dishtowel.
We tumble out into the magic
together everyday
and you don't seem to
mind I trip wherever we go.

LOOK 8 2020 PP

5/4/13

Sometimes I'm whole
and can conceive
of being seamless.
Other times I'm fractured
and can only try to remember
how sorrow brings you closer. At the end of the sit
the bowl is struck
and the waves blow away
the sand pile that is me
leaving only an outline of light
that I roll up like yarn
then laugh, "Now what am I?"
Nothing and everything
joy and sorrow.

LOOK 4 FP 2020

Can't explain

This sadness
will never leave.
It slides down windows
it clogs up drains
it flies around me like red leaves before a cold rain.

Still a quiet faith
just keeps hanging on
it laughs at my tears
it writes me a song
it points the way saying slowly.

This daydreaming heart that falls up stairs
it bangs down streets, it cuts my hair, like January
slush that splashes in shoes it smells like snow.

Ultra marine sky
holding out arms to the day
share your peace with us
remind me how we've changed.

Thank you for keeping me
safe with you
through all the weather
and being true
these prayers send you love always.

Living at the edge of the gorge
your strong heart made the whole thing roll
your devotion kept the hounds from the door
I tried to keep above the storm
and always be there for you

Still this sadness
will never leave
an old bone
of what has been
an old break, a tired grin

together we begin again.

Nowhere to run

Learning to stand in the uncertainty,
learning to sit with the silence.

The stillness has surprises if you don't run away -
patience, compassion, understanding
and visits from the One.

Learning to listen
to the flowing truth
learning to hear the songs.
Life is full of miracles
I know because I've seen them.
The light dawns from within you!
And the One responds.

LOOK 24 PP 2020

In the dream

When I lay down to sleep in my dream
I wake up here.

When I wake up here we do all this
and get to touch.

When the bearers
come down the hill with the stretcher
to collect the body
my body -

when they pick up the body there
I wake up here.

LOOK 31 [illegible]P 2020

Finding silence in the crowd

What's happening is this:
Any fear
is my own addition.
Because if it's meant for you
it's coming
and I know it.
Blue-green rain
wrapping me up in this emerald city
I wake up to
find myself asleep at your feet
somehow wrapped in a blanket
that finally, no one can take away.

The important thing

Instead of
one day at a time how about
inhale to exhale
or paradigm shift
to quantum leap or how to exist
as a square within a rolling sphere?
Be the answer
for someone - remember
we're in motion and destined
to soar.

LOOK 13 PP 2020

3rd and Pine

In the gray
of the early city
I try to divine the formula
for staying upright.
Nothing comes until I see you walking toward me
and the Source speaks:
Trust in me every moment,
in every step.
and life is transformed

Hail the rising of our heart

In the mystical light of dusk
we send up our breath to the first star

The blessings are with you
don't doubt them.
We run toward the heart of knowing
the great expanse all around us.
Oh this bittersweet life
it has a mind of its own.

Snow blankets the city

I watch you watching the snow
and want you to know
know that one person
has dedicated their life to you.

One person
has experienced all dreams come true
in the hours spent with you,
has defined a perfect day
in spending simple moments with you.

We throw our offering
into the river together, the sunflowers racing
a trail to our future.

There's no separation could divide us
except the one we could create.
There's no sadness could destroy us
unless we forget today.

If there is suffering
then open your hand
if there is doubt
then walk until it passes
these are only shadow.

Our miracle is here.

One pointed zero

The mantra in the silence
spins like a prayer wheel
in the darkness of my mind.
Creating sparks, calling me
to not wander off.

LOOK 30 PP 2020

The crane

What is life?
I'm drifting in it
at a temperature that is something between inner
and outer wildfire.
It has to do with light and sound.
I am light and sound.
There's a pattern here says life
See how I'm always on the move
like roots, like breath, like tides.
I used to miss home then
realized there's no reason
what's really the difference between here and there?
We're all brothers and sisters, mothers and fathers
long lost lovers.
Flying along here
living all
already gone.

Tanya and Peter Parks, 2021

...

www.ingramcontent.com/pod-product-compliance
Lightning Source LLC
LaVergne TN
LVHW052052160826
845678LV00015B/3190

* 9 7 8 0 5 7 8 8 1 4 9 0 2 *